For Lolo.
—D. D.

For E.
—M. I.

PHILOMEL BOOKS
An imprint of Penguin Random House LLC, New York

First published in the United States of America by Philomel Books,
an imprint of Penguin Random House LLC, 2021.

Text copyright © 2021 by Drew Daywalt
Illustrations copyright © 2021 by Molly Idle

Visit us online at penguinrandomhouse.com.

Library of Congress Cataloging-in-Publication Data is available.

Manufactured in China

ISBN 9780399171321

10 9 8 7 6 5 4 3 2 1

Edited by Jill Santopolo.
Designed by Ellice M. Lee.
Text set in Bell MT Pro.
Art done in Prismacolor pencil on paper.

Words by Drew Daywalt
Pictures by Molly Idle

PHILOMEL

One night, Clyde noticed one little

star all alone in the big black blanket of night above.

He stared at the star for a long time, then said,

"Star light, star bright,

The first star I see tonight . . .

I wish I may, I wish I might,

Have the wish I wish tonight.

I wish for a . . ."

And then, at that very moment, Clyde closed his eyes

and wished as hard as he could. His wish was a secret.

He opened his eyes and looked around, hoping his wish had come true, but it hadn't. With a sigh, he stood up and walked home.

And that is how it came to be that
Clyde and Star granted each other's
wishes, became best friends, and were
never ever lonely again.

THE END